A Tempting Tatum Novella

Unwrapping Tatum

NEW YORK TIMES AND USA TODAY BESTSELLING AUTHOR

KAYLEE RYAN

Cover Design: Pink Ink Designs
Cover Photography: Shutterstock
Editing: Hot Tree Editing
Formatting: Integrity Formatting

DEDICATION

To my readers.

Thank you for loving Tatum and Blaise

CHAPTER 1

BLAISE

My eyes flutter open as the pale morning light drifts in through the windows. The feel of her soft hands on my chest lets me know she's awake too. I hold her a little tighter, for no other reason except that I can. We've been married going on four years now, and yet this moment, waking up next to her, never ceases to cause my heart to skip a beat.

I wish I could say that this is the highlight of my day, but that would be a lie. Every minute is a constant highlight reel. Sure, we have our arguments just like all married couples, but they are few and far between.

"Hey, you," I say, my voice husky from sleep.

"Morning, B." She kisses my chest.

I hear the pitter-patter of little feet and know it's only a matter of time before our twins, Gavin and Addyson, make themselves known. It's the first Saturday in December, and we promised them that today we would go see Santa. They've been looking forward to this all week.

"How long do you think they'll hold out?"

She laughs softly. "We have five minutes tops."

"Then we better make it count."

Tatum rises up on her elbows and I meet her halfway, my lips molding to hers. She knows I refuse to get out of bed until I've kissed her thoroughly. It's our thing.

"Five minutes is more than enough time to try for baby number three," I murmur against her lips.

"Wow, five minutes. It sucks getting old."

I can feel her smile against my lips. "I'll show you old," I say, flipping her over so I'm hovering over her. "I love you, Mrs. Richards." I bend to capture her lips as I grind my hips into her.

"Today's the day, right, Daddy?"

"We get to see Santa?"

Addyson and Gavin come barreling into the room and bounce on the bed. I rest my forehead against Tate's, trying to get myself under control to greet my kids. Rolling off her, I prop myself up on my elbow, pulling the covers over my waist to hide what their mother does to me. They're still a bit young for the birds and bees conversation.

"That's right. Today's the day we go see Santa. But first, we have to have breakfast. What sounds good?" Tate asks them.

"Pancakes!" they yell in unison.

"All right, you two, pancakes it is. Are your rooms

picked up? Santa will know if they're not. He might even ask you, and you want to be able to say yes, right?" I ask them.

Their little heads bob up and down and then they're off. I wait until I hear them down the hall before leaning down to kiss Tate again. "Tonight," I say against her lips. "We work on baby number three tonight."

"Tonight," she agrees.

One more quick kiss and I force myself out of bed, Tate following. It's time to make the munchkins some pancakes and go visit Santa.

CHAPTER 2

"Are we there yet?" Addyson asks excitedly.

"Yeah, are we?" Gavin chimes in.

I look over at Blaise in the driver seat and see his grin is just as wide as mine. We both knew we wanted kids. It happened a little sooner than we expected, but I wouldn't change it for anything. I never thought they would bring this much joy to my life. I love getting to see the world for the first time through them.

"Almost. Maybe another five minutes," Blaise answers. Reaching over, he laces his fingers through mine and we listen to the twins chatter about what they're going to ask Santa for this year.

The mall parking lot is packed, not that we expected otherwise. It always is this time of year. "All right, you two. You ready to go see Santa?" I ask, taking off my seat belt. They respond with cheers and clapping. Without looking back, I know they're trying to get out of their seats.

Blaise reaches in and unbuckles Gavin while I unbuckle Addyson. "Hold my hand. We're in a parking lot," I remind her.

"Okay, okay, let's go," she says, gripping my hand and trying to pull me toward the back of the truck. I let her but only a few feet, and then we wait for the boys to catch up. Addyson immediately reaches for Gavin's hand and the four of us head inside.

"The line's not as bad as I thought it would be," Blaise comments.

"I know. I was hoping that getting an early start would help us miss the crowds."

"So, you think she'll do it this year?" he asks, nodding toward our daughter.

"I don't know. She's pretty excited." Addyson has never been a big fan of sitting on Santa's lap. Last year, it took a lot of coaxing until finally, she stood beside Gavin where he was perched on Santa's knee.

"That she is." He laughs. "They both are."

"Daddy, you think Santa will really bring us new bikes?" Addyson asks him.

Blaise bends down so he is eye level with both of them. "Is that what you really want?"

"Yes!" they say in unison. "And we're going to get rid of the little wheels too, right, Daddy? You said you would help us."

Blaise chuckles and so do I. "The training wheels, and yes, I'll help you. We both will, but there's nothing wrong with training wheels. They help you learn balance. And remember that everyone learns at their own pace," he reminds them.

"Like that's going to dim their competitive spark." I laugh.

Blaise looks up at me and winks. "You guys are up next. Are you ready?"

Their little heads bob up and down. So far Addyson is showing no fear. That's a good sign. I watch as my man's man husband, still crouching, pulls our kids into his arms and gives them both a big hug.

"You want Daddy to go with you?"

He's looking at Addyson. I swear she has him wrapped around her little finger. They both do, but his little girl bats those eyelashes and he's done for.

"Daaadd," Gavin whines. "We can do it."

"What about you, sweet pea? You want Daddy to go with you?" he asks Addyson.

She shakes her head. "Bubby and me can go together," she says, reaching for Gavin. He takes her hand and they turn to face the front of the line, effectively dismissing Blaise.

"Damn," he says as he stands and puts his arm around my waist. "They're growing up too fast, Tate. We need to get busy on baby number three."

"Rome wasn't built in a day," I say, trying to suppress my grin.

"Is that a challenge, Mrs. Richards?" he whispers huskily.

"You up for it?"

He pulls me so that I'm standing in front of him, my back against his chest. With a slight tip of his hips, I can feel what our little exchange has done to him. "I'm up for you," he says against my ear.

I don't reply as the twins are next and making their way toward Santa. Blaise grabs Gavin's coat from my arms and carries it to hide the evidence as we walk behind them and stop just beside the red carpet that leads to his chair. I hold my breath as I watch them each take a knee, neither one showing fear. I hear Blaise exhale from beside me.

"She's doing great," he says. I can hear the happiness in his voice. He can't take it when either of them is upset. I often find myself having to dish out the punishments because my tattoo artist husband is too weak when it comes to our children.

We stand side by side and watch as our two little miracles, a piece of each of us, smile as they tell Santa what they want for Christmas.

"Do you want a picture?" one of the elves asks.

"Yes." Blaise hands me Gavin's coat and reaches for his wallet. "We need five, please," he says, handing over his debit card.

I don't bother asking why we need so many; I already know. The twins—as well as their cousin, Brandon, and Leah's daughter, Sophie—are spoiled rotten by our friends and family. We get a copy, as do his parents as well as Ember, Asher, and Leah. He knows we would never hear the end of it if they each didn't get their own. On the flip side, we're the same way when it comes to

Brandon and Sophie. We're a tight-knit group.

The elf snaps the picture, Santa hands the kids a candy cane, and just like that this year's Santa meet and greet was a success.

"Look," they say at the same time. They do that a lot. Of course, I should be used to it since Blaise and Asher do the same thing. It's a little freaky at times.

"I see. We'll have to save them for later," I say. The mom in me doesn't want them to be a sticky mess for the ride home.

Blaise scoops them both up, one in each arm. "I'm so proud of both of you. You did great."

"I asked for a bike," Addyson says proudly.

"Me too. A big-kid bike," Gavin chimes in.

"Well, I can vouch that you both have been very good this year," Blaise says.

"All right, you three. What are we going to do with the rest of our day?" I ask, even though I already know. We're going to Blaise's parents to make Christmas cookies. The whole gang is going to be there. We just didn't tell the kids.

"Ice cream!" the twins suggest with too much glee for December.

Blaise chuckles. "Not today, but I think what Mommy and I have planned will be even better," he assures them.

CHAPTER 3

BLAISE

As soon as I turn on Mom and Dad's road, the twins are cheering in the backseat. They love coming to Grandma and Grandpa's. Sometimes I can see the sadness in Tate's eyes when they do. I know she misses her parents, even more so around the holidays. I hope the gift I have planned for her, which in turn is kind of for the twins as well, will be well received.

"Is Sophie here, Mommy?" Addyson asks.

"Yeah, and Brandon? We can play trucks," Gavin says.

I pull up behind Asher's truck and park. Tate takes off her seat belt and turns to face the twins. "They're both here. Grandma wants to make Christmas cookies. You think you can help her with that?"

"Yes!" they say in unison.

"Well, we better not keep them waiting."

Before Tate and I can get out of the truck, Addyson

and Gavin are already bouncing in their seats and unstrapping the buckles. After her parents' accident, and subsequently hers, she's as strict as am I about car seats and seat belts. The twins know that they have to stay in their seats until Mom and Dad are out of the car, unless told otherwise.

As soon as their little feet hit the ground, they are off at a dead run into the house. My dad opens the door just in time and they attach themselves to his legs.

"Grandpa!"

"Well, look at you two, all dressed up. Did you have a hot date today or something?" he asks them.

"Ewww. No, we went to see Santa," Gavin says.

"Well, did you tell him I said hello?"

Addyson gasps. "You know Santa?" she asks. You can hear the awe in her voice.

"Of course I do. Santa and I go way back," he tells her.

"Can you tell him we've been super-duper good?" Gavin asks.

"Yeah, cuz we want big-kid bikes," Addyson informs him.

"And Daddy's gonna show us to not use the little wheels," Gavin chimes in.

Dad chuckles. "I'll see what I can do. Now, Grandma's in the house with Sophie and Brandon. They're waiting on the two of you to help them makes some cookies."

"And there they go." I laugh as Tate and I step up onto the porch.

"Those two are full of energy. Come on in out of the cold," Dad says. He snakes his arm out as Tate walks by and kisses her cheek.

In the house, Asher, Brent, and Jackson are watching football in the living room. I assume that's where Dad was as well. Tate heads toward the kitchen and I detour to go hang with the guys.

"How was Santa?" Asher asks.

"Good. Addy didn't cry this year. We got pictures out in the truck."

"I thought for sure Soph was going to lose her shit, but she held strong," Brent says. "She was a little teary-eyed when she approached him, but by the time it was over, she was all smiles."

"No trouble on our end." Asher laughs. "Brandon ran up to him, hopped up on a knee and started yanking on his beard."

"Gavin has always pretty much been the same way, but Addy, she was not too impressed last year."

"I remember," Dad says. "That picture was epic."

"I had to walk away. I can't handle the tears," I admit.

"Tell me about it," Brent says. "At least when they get older Gavin will help even the score. I have two women in my household."

"You know you have a fifty-fifty chance of fixing that, right?" Asher asks.

"Working on it, my man. Working on it." Brent grins.

"And you." I point to Jackson. "How long are you and Ember going to wait to make us uncles again?"

Jackson shrugs. "If it were up to me, you already would be. Em says she wants to enjoy being married for a while before we add kids to the mix."

"You've been married for what, two years now?" Brent asks.

"Yeah, next week. I don't want to rush her, and being Uncle Jackson is great, but honestly I want to upgrade that title soon."

"She'll get there," Dad says. "Ember has always had her own timeline, marched to the beat of her own drum. Hell, I think the only time she's not lived by that was when she wanted her tattoos and these two"—he points to me and Asher—"made her wait to finish college."

"True," Asher and I say at the same time. Everyone laughs.

"So listen, I know I'm running out of time—" I look back at the door and drop my voice. "—but well, I have an idea for Tate, and kind of for the twins for Christmas. You guys feel like taking a ride with me?

They all agree and we head off to tell our wives that we're going out. When we reach the kitchen, Mom and Gavin are mixing dough, Ember and Addy are rolling out dough, Leah and Sophie are cutting cookies, and Grace and Brandon, who just turned two, are attempting to decorate cookies. Tate is just standing back with a watery smile on her face, taking it all in.

"Hey, you," I say, wrapping my arms around her.

"You okay?"

"Yeah, just memorizing the moment," she replies, laying her hands over mine.

"Don't get so caught up in memorizing that you miss the fun."

"Oh trust me, I won't. I'm the relief. One of them"—she points to the women—"is going to need a break. I'm thinking Grace is going to be the first."

I look over and see Brandon with his hand in his mouth and icing all over his face. "I think you're right." I laugh. "Hey, the guys and I are going to go do some shopping. You good here?"

"You know we are. Look for the you know. . . ." She tilts her head toward the twins.

"Will do, baby. We'll be back soon."

She turns to face me and I kiss her lips.

"Love you, B," she whispers.

"Love you too."

CHAPTER 4

I wait until I see the truck pull out of the drive and then turn to face my partners in crime. "I didn't think they were ever going to get him out of the house."

Addy gasps. "Mommy, that's not nice," she scolds me.

I hold back my grin. "I know, baby girl, but Mommy wants to surprise Daddy for Christmas, and I need Grandma's and your aunts' help."

"Oh!" Her eyes go wide. "I want to help."

"You will, but it's a secret. You can't tell anyone."

Her little head bobs up and down. "I can keep secrets."

"Good. Now let's make some cookies."

We rush through getting the next batch in the oven, and then Nancy suggests that the kids take a break from all of their hard work and watch some cartoons. This of course was an easy sell. Grace goes to put Brandon down for a nap, Ember gets the TV fired up while Nancy, Leah and I get juice boxes and fruit snacks for the kids.

"Okay, we're good," Ember says, pulling us back into the kitchen. "Now, what's the grand plan of yours? Just the fact that we had to get my brother out of the house has me on pins and needles."

"Well, Blaise and I have been trying for another." I point to the living room, keeping my voice low. Little ears tend to hear everything.

"We know," they all say.

"He doesn't exactly hide the fact." Nancy laughs.

"True. Well anyway, I went to the doctor earlier this week and it looks like he's getting his Christmas wish."

After a round of hugs and congratulations, I tell them my plan.

"I'm in," Ember says. "I love the idea."

"Thanks, but I need all of your help. It's not easy hiding anything from him."

"Oh, but I'm sure it's not exactly a hardship, I mean, he does still think you all are trying." Leah wags her eyebrows.

I can feel my face heat with embarrassment.

"None of that." Nancy points to my obviously red face. "I say enjoy it."

Everyone cracks up at that, including me. I'm blessed to have found this family. I would like to think that my parents had something to do with it, although Leah and Brent really should get most of the credit.

"It's awful quiet in there." Leah points over her shoulder.

"I'll go check it out. I need to check on Brandon anyway," Grace says.

"So what day were you thinking?" Nancy asks.

"Well, I thought Christmas Eve. We'll all be here anyway, so I figured why not."

"That's perfect," Ember beams.

"So yeah, they're all crashed on the couch. Brandon is still snoozing away too," Grace says, joining us. "Let's hammer out the details."

We spend the next hour putting my plan in motion. It's going to be hard to hold this to myself for the next four weeks, but I hope the surprise will be worth it. He did say he wanted a baby for Christmas.

CHAPTER 5

BLAISE

"So what exactly are we doing?" Asher asks me.

"I need some help with a few things in the attic."

"Her parents' stuff," Brent says. He's more observant of our wives than I thought.

"When she committed to staying here in Tennessee, we had it all moved here. She didn't go through it, just simply rented a new unit and told the movers to load it up. She brought all the pictures and home movies here." I point to my house as we pull into the drive. "I need your help going through the movies and pictures. I want to create a new home movie with clips from theirs as well as still shots. The twins should know their other grandparents as more than just a picture on the mantel."

"Is she going to be okay with this?" Dad asks.

"I hope so. I mean, I know she wants the kids to know them, and she misses them like crazy. We have a few pictures at the house, but I think it needs to be more than that."

"Damn," Asher says. "You're going to make her cry, bro. Can you handle that?"

I think about it for a few minutes. "Yeah. I mean, I know there will be tears, but honestly, I think she needs that. The holidays are hard for her and even though her parents are gone, they're not forgotten. She's hiding from the pain, but in the long run, I think it'll do her some good to share this with the twins."

"Shit, I need to rethink the earrings I got Ember," Jackson tries to lighten the mood, and it works.

"We all do," Asher grumbles.

"You guys in or not?"

"Do you even have to ask? I mean this is Tate we're talking about. Of course we are," Dad says.

Climbing out of the truck, I lead them inside and into the garage where the attic entrance is. "We've got a lot to cover in a short amount of time."

"Lead the way, my man," Jackson says.

We spend the next two hours sifting through boxes of pictures. Pictures of my wife when she was a little girl. Addy looks just like her. Seeing that just reinforces that this is the right thing. She needs to share this part of her life, of who she is. We need to remember them every damn day.

"How about we take the movies to the shop? We can watch them there. I assume that's where you were planning on putting this together?" Asher asks.

"Yeah, I figured that would be the easiest place. Here

is not an option, and being anywhere else for hours at a time would raise a red flag."

"You need to block out your schedule at the shop. Take a day or two to sift through it all," Asher suggests.

"I hate to leave that on you, man."

"This is a slow time of year. Everyone busy with the holidays. I can handle it. We might have to pull you away for a walk-in, but I would block any open spots you have and get this done."

That's the great thing about owning your own business—Asher and I make our schedules. We scheduled hours Monday–Friday noon to five. This is where walk-ins are welcome if the schedule isn't full. All other times are by appointment only. We do weekends by appointment, as well as evenings. It's a hell of a lot easier to manage our busy lives this way, especially now we have kids.

"Okay, so we also need a real shopping day. I obviously need to step up my game," Jackson says again.

"Not a bad idea," Brent agrees. "Blaise, you can say you're with us, but be at the shop. If you get busted, just say you had a last-minute call or something."

"You guys are too good at this shit. Should I be worried?"

They all laugh, but really they're getting into this.

"All right, we better get back. I'd say they've had as much cookie making as they can handle." Dad laughs.

"Hey!" Asher mocks being offended. "Those are your grandkids you're talking about."

"And I love them with everything in me, but those little buggers can wear you down fast."

"We got your back, old man." I place my hand on his shoulder.

"Heathens, I tell you." He grins.

After loading up the boxes of movies and the pictures I'm going to use, we stop by the shop to drop them off and then head back to Mom and Dad's.

When Dad opens the door, we're greeted with silence. I can hear the low hum of cartoons coming from the living room and the faint whisper of our wives from the kitchen.

"So much for needing relief," Brent says as we enter the kitchen.

Five heads snap toward the door. Looks like we might have interrupted something.

"Ladies," Jackson says, making his way to Ember.

"We didn't expect you back so soon," Mom says in greeting.

"We can see that." Dad kisses her cheek. "What did you do to my grandbabies, put them in a sugar coma?"

"They worked their little hearts out. It was time for a snack break."

"You know, Mom, there are child labor laws." Asher tries to sound stern, but the big-ass grin on his face gives him away.

"Oh hush. How was shopping?" she asks.

Brent shrugs. "I'm going to need to go again."

"Me too," Jackson chimes in. "Didn't find exactly what I was looking for."

Mom takes her time looking at each one of us before glancing at the girls. "Mischief, I tell you. Pure mischief."

We erupt in laughter, which ends the nap. Gavin crawls up in my lap and Addy in Jackson's.

"What's funny?" Sophie asks, going to Brent.

"Nothing, sweetheart. Grandma was just being silly."

"Is it time for more cookies?" Addy asks.

"Not today, baby girl. It's time to go home."

"Let them stay," Mom says. She turns to look at Dad, and he nods. "How about a sleepover?"

The kids cheer and Dad winks. "Off you go. We got this. Go do some shopping or make babies, whatever it is you need to do."

"Gramps, where do babies come from?" Sophie asks him.

"A very special place made with more love than you can handle," Mom answers for him.

After they convince us to leave all four kids, we say our good-byes and head out. I wave over my shoulder at them, and they us. None of us makes plans to get together for a kid-free night. This opportunity doesn't come along very often, and I'm sure we're all going to use our time wisely. Jackson and Ember don't even linger.

CHAPTER 6

We're driving home and it's quiet. Too quiet without the chatter of the kids. It's giving me time to think, and the only conclusion I can come up with is that I'm going to hell. I saw the look in Blaise's eyes when his parents offered to keep the kids. I know that he's going to cash in on his promise from this morning to work on baby number three. I should tell him. It's wrong to keep it from him, but this surprise I have planned, it's good. At least I think it is.

Blaise parks the truck and throws off his seat belt. He leans over the console, places one hand on the back of my neck, the other on my thigh, and pulls me into a kiss. "So sweet," he whispers. "I believe I have a promise to keep." He kisses me one more time, releases me and hops out of the truck. My head is still swimming from the kiss, so I'm startled when he opens my door. He doesn't say a word, just reaches in, unhooks my belt and slides his arms around me, one behind my back and one under my ass, lifting me out of the truck. Closing the door with his hip, he carries me up the front steps.

"I can walk, Blaise."

"I know you can, but I like you in my arms."

Every day. Every single day he's like this. He never hesitates to show me or the kids how much he adores us. All the more reason to make my telling him about the pregnancy something special. We found out about the twins when I was in the hospital, so I didn't get to see the wonder in his eyes when he found out. Sure he was thrilled, but I missed that. I want it this time around.

We reach the front door and he carefully sets me on my feet.

"Didn't think that through did you, Prince Charming?"

"No. I'll admit all I wanted was you in my arms." He makes quick work of unlocking the door and holding it open for me. I hear the door shut, the lock click into place, and then I'm suddenly weightless again as he scoops me up with what feels like no effort and marches to our room.

He sets me on the bed, and I can't help but tease him. I glance over at the clock. "Five minutes, right?"

He chuckles. "Baby, you'll be lucky if I'm done with you in five hours."

"Promises, promises," I breathe against his lips.

"You know I always keep my promises."

"I might need you to convince me," I say between kisses.

"Challenge accepted." He slides from the bed and then reaches for me. I place my hand in his and allow him to help me stand. Slowly, painstakingly so, he removes all of my clothes piece by piece, his lips tracing every new inch of exposed skin.

"Blaise." His name is part moan and part whisper as it falls from my lips. He smirks, knowing he's driving me crazy. My eyes follow his every move as he strips out of his clothes, thankfully faster than he rid me of mine.

"Bed," he says, his silver eyes raking over my naked body.

Not wanting to delay whatever it is he has planned, I take my spot on the bed, right in the middle, ready and waiting for him.

"So pretty," he says as he runs his finger over my center. "And wet," he murmurs as he settles over me. I'm just about to tell him he's not very good at convincing when suddenly he's everywhere. Hands, lips, teeth. He kneads my breast with one hand while taking the other between his teeth. He nips and then soothes it with his tongue, trailing kisses up my neck. I tilt my head, giving him full access. When I feel his lips leave my skin, I groan in protest. Opening my eyes, I see him hovering over me, eyes sparking with desire. "Hey, you," he whispers as his lips softly meld against mine.

"More," I mumble.

"I'm going to get it right this time, Tate. I'm going to make love to you and we're going to get baby number three," he vows.

The words are on the tip of my tongue to tell him. I know how bad he wants this. Then he pushes inside me and all thoughts of what I should do leave my mind. All I can do is feel. It's always been this way with us; he consumes me, and it's just us. Sliding my arms under his, I run my hands up and down his back.

"Love you," he whispers, kissing me again, his tongue tracing my lips.

"Love you too, B."

Slowly, ever so slowly, he swivels his hips. Suddenly slow is not going to work for me. I need him. I wrap my legs around his waist and pull him into me, causing him to chuckle.

"Greedy," he says, sucking a nipple into his mouth.

"Please." I'm not against begging for what I want. Not to mention he can't say no to me. It's not something I take advantage of often, but in the bedroom, all bets are off.

"What do you need, sweets?"

"You . . . more . . . please," I say breathlessly.

"This?" He rocks his hips into me.

I close my eyes and just feel. Everywhere, I feel him. "I'm close," I say, raising my hips to meet his.

"Together," he growls, and that sends me over the edge.

I wrap my arms around him and pull him into me. I love the feel of his weight on me.

"I'll crush you, Tate." He tries to lift up on his elbows.

"No. Stay, please." I know he will. It's that "never denying me" thing again. Once I have my breathing under control, I open my eyes and find his silver orbs watching me. "I'd say you got your wish."

He chuckles. "I know it will happen, but I'm having a hell of a time practicing until it does." He winks.

I look over at the clock. "Not quite five hours, but more than five minutes," I tease him.

"Oh sweets, I'm not through with you."

He spends the rest of the night showing me how he keeps his promises.

CHAPTER 7

BLAISE

Waking up to a quiet house has me missing the twins. Don't get me wrong, I enjoyed the hell out of my wife last night. Speaking of my wife, I made love to her this morning, something we don't get to do much of these days. The twins are early risers.

"Can we go shopping before we pick them up? I want to get their bikes," Tate says from her seat across from me at the kitchen table.

"Yeah. I talked to Mom and she said they're having a Christmas movie day and eating the cookies they made yesterday."

"It shouldn't take long. Where are we going to keep them?"

I'll put them out in the attached garage. The kids are never out there, especially this time of year."

"I'll go shower." She stands and takes her plate to the sink.

"I'll—"

"No sir, you will not. We will never get out of here if you join me. I'll be fast, I promise." She leans in for a quick kiss. I try to hold her against me, but she breaks free, laughing as she runs to the bedroom.

"So other than big-kid bikes, what are you thinking?" I ask Tate as we venture into the toy store.

"Gavin wants blocks, and Addy asked for a new baby doll. I guess it pees."

"Okay, let's do this," I say, grabbing a cart.

The first aisle is board games. I grab Whack-A-Mole and throw it in the cart. And because I know we like to be even with gifts to open, I throw in Connect Four as well. "They're old enough for this now, right?" I ask, pointing to the cart.

"What does the box say?"

I grab the game and read the box. "Says ages six and up." I toss it back in.

"They're going to be four, Blaise."

"I know, and they're already too smart for their own good. They can do this easy peasy."

She just smiles and shakes her head. "Okay, time for baby dolls."

I roll the cart down the aisle, and there is a doll that looks just like Addy and Tate. Long dark wavy hair and big green eyes. I pick it up and toss it in the cart as well.

"Babe, that's not the one she asked for."

I shrug. "Yeah, but it looks like my girls, so she needs it."

"Needs it, huh?" She laughs.

"Yep."

"There." Tate points to a doll on my side of the aisle. I grab it from the shelf and add it to the cart. At the end of the aisle, there's a baby stroller, carrier, and all kinds of baby stuff in a set, so I grab that too.

"She has a stroller." Tate laughs.

"Yeah, but look at all that other stuff in there. She's going to love it."

"You spoil them," she chides me.

I don't deny it. They're my babies; of course I spoil them. "Where are these blocks that little man asked for?"

"A few aisles over is where the boy stuff starts." Tate places her hand on the small of my back and pushes me forward. "Those." She points to a set of Lincoln Logs. "I know he wants those, and then there was a big bag of the bigger-size Legos he asked for too."

I grab the Lincoln Logs and toss them in the cart. At the end of the aisle, Tate finds the big bag of Legos. "We're making quick work of this, sweets." I lean down, my lips next to her ear. "We had time for a round in the shower." I kiss her temple before standing to my full height once more.

"Impossible." She grins.

We add a few trucks to the cart. In the center aisle, there is a Barbie Jeep that I know Addy will love, so I toss that in too.

"Okay, we need stocking stuffers."

I push the cart toward two aisles filled with smaller trinkets and see all kinds of things the twins will love. I grab a few for each.

"Well, that takes care of that. Now the bikes."

The bikes are in the back of the store, so I have to turn the cart around and head the other direction. At the end of the aisle are the matching pink and blue bikes adorned with training wheels that they asked for. Tate grabs a tag from each one so we can take it to the register with us. I move over to the next aisle and grab a blue and pink basket and a bell for each. My kids' rides must be pimped. I meet Tate again at the end of the aisle. She notices the baskets and grins.

"You, my dear husband, are like a big kid yourself. I should have left you at home," she teases.

"Hell no, this is too much fun. We get to live vicariously through them."

"You're doing a great job of that, B." She bumps her shoulder into mine. "I think we're good. I already have a few things for them at home, pajamas and things like that."

"All right, then." I point the cart toward the checkout counter. Once we pay, the cashier radios someone in the back to bring the bikes around. I take the cart outside and pull the truck up while Tate waits.

Once everything is loaded and we're on our way back to the house, I reach over and take her hand in mine. "We make a good team, Tatum Richards."

"That we do."

CHAPTER 8

I never went back to work once the twins were born. It was a big decision for us, but financially we were good, so Blaise and I decided that this was the best decision for our family. Looking back now, I'm glad I did. I love my time with the kids, and we get to go have lunch with Blaise and Asher at the shop. Grace and I help cover the receptionist when she needs days off, each of us taking turns watching the others kids.

Today, however, she and I are in full planning mode. I've called in the troops for lunch, Leah, Ember, and Grace. Blaise's parents have the kids. I used to feel guilty asking them until the one time I didn't, and they were crushed. They're both retired now and live for the times the house is filled with their grandkids. I want to run through the plans for Blaise's surprise one more time. We told the guys we were shopping; however, Asher, Brent, and Jackson are all in on the plan now. Even my father-in-law. They have all been sworn to secrecy, and they love the fact that they know something Blaise doesn't.

"I think we've got it," Leah says, sitting back in her chair.

"You think so?" I ask. I still feel bad for holding onto the news.

"Yeah, I'll make up the cards," Ember says. "It will be easier for me with no little ones around to hide it from."

"And just when are you going to do something about that?" Grace asks her.

She blushes. Ember doesn't blush. "I hope soon. I know Jackson has been wanting to for a while. I thought maybe I can tell him that I stopped taking my birth control for his Christmas present. Is that too cheesy?"

"Hell no, not if it's something he wants," Leah tells her.

"It is," I confirm. "I guess Blaise asked him the same question and he pretty much said he was waiting for you to be ready. At least that's the story I got from my husband," I tell her.

"I need to think of a way . . . something cool like what you're doing to tell him," Ember says, her eyes filled with excitement.

"Wrap up your pills, and add a Marvin Gaye CD to the package," Grace says.

We all sing the famous line from "Let's Get it On."

"Seriously? That's the best you've got?" Ember asks.

"Honestly, yes," Leah says. "Sometimes less is more. And if he decides that he's not actually ready, then you can laugh about Marvin and use the CD to get some practice in." She waggles her eyebrows.

"You know what? Maybe you're right. Simple is good, and I like the idea of being able to laugh it off if he's changed his mind," Ember agrees.

"He's not going to change his mind. He may not be one of the Richards men, but he might as well be. It does something primal to them to know they knocked you up." Grace laughs.

"That's exactly why my brother is not going to be mad at you. Hell, we all know he wants another one, and this plan of yours is epic," Ember assures me.

"I hope you're right." My hope is that Blaise will be so excited that he'll easily overlook the fact that I will have known about this pregnancy for four weeks by the time he finds out. Hopefully he'll see all the thought I put into revealing the news.

"Come on, this is Blaise we're talking about," Leah says. "Has he ever been mad at you?" she asks.

"Doubtful." Grace chuckles.

"Hey, it's not like your husbands don't treat you the same," I fire back.

"You're right. They do. That's why we know it's all going to be okay." Grace places her hand over mine.

"Right. Okay, so Ember, you have the notes for the cards. You all know your part."

"Yes. I'll tell Mom and Dad theirs as well. That's one less thing you have to do, and you don't have to worry about little ears when you call," Ember volunteers.

"They're going to be so excited that they get to help. No way can I tell them now. They would spill the beans in a heartbeat."

Grace's phone beeps. We watch as she pulls it out of her purse. "It's Asher. They're done at the shop. He's on his way home."

"All right, ladies. Looks like this meeting of the minds is over. Tate, it's going to be amazing." Leah stands and gives me a hug. "I'm so happy for you guys."

After a round of hugs and more of the same sentiments, we all head our separate ways. We have a solid plan and I can't help but be excited.

They're right. Blaise will be too thrilled to be upset.

CHAPTER 9

BLAISE

"How does your schedule look today?" Tatum asks as she loads the dishwasher. We just finished breakfast.

"Full day," I lie. Technically I do have a full day, but not of clients. But it's a lie all the same, and I never lie to her.

"Okay. I was going to bring the kids by for lunch, but maybe we'll do it another day."

Damn. Shit. Fuck. "Yeah, I don't know how long each piece is going to take. I would hate for you to lug the kids out and me not be able to stop and see you." I'm a prick.

"Hey." She dries her hands and steps in to me where I'm leaning against the counter. "We know you're busy. Wipe the frown off your face. It's not a big deal, B. We'll see you when you get home. If something changes, call me." She stands on her tiptoes and presses her lips to mine.

I snake my arms around her waist and hold her tight

against me. I instantly relax; it's not a lie but a secret. A secret for her, anyway. One I hope that she loves. If I'm being honest, a little of my anxiety is about how she's going to take it. I hope that going through her movies and pictures doesn't upset her. I've been working on it for the last two weeks, and the guys have all helped. I'm just as much excited as I am nervous to give it to her.

"Love you," I say, resting my forehead against her.

"Love you too."

"I need to get going," I tell her, not making any effort to move away from her.

Tate finally pulls away. "Hey, guys!" she yells into the living room. "Daddy's gotta leave for work."

I hear two loud thuds and the tromping of little feet as they race into the kitchen. "Daddy!" they yell, each one crashing into a leg.

My heart fucking swells. I never knew I was capable of loving this much, not until Tatum. Then we found out we were having twins and I was scared as hell, but excited too. I can still remember the minute I heard them cry for the first time. It's an experience and a love like no other.

I crouch down and wrap an arm around each of them. "You two need to be good for Mommy today. I'll see you later." I kiss Addy on the cheek and then Gavin. "I love you," I tell them.

"Bye, Daddy. We love you."

Just like that, they're racing back to the living room to finish watching their cartoons.

"So much energy." Tate smiles.

"Come here." I reach out for her hand, and she takes mine as I pull her back into my chest. "I'll see you later, beautiful." I kiss her, nipping at her bottom lip. All too soon I pull away, grab my keys and head out.

When I get to the shop, the Closed sign is still turned. However, I see Asher's truck in the parking lot. Digging my keys out of my pocket, I unlock the door. I can hear him and Grace talking back in the office. It's a large room that we share.

"Hey, what's going on?" I ask, sitting at my desk and firing up my computer.

"I didn't have anything on the books today and Grace offered to help with the video."

"It's a great idea, Blaise. She's going to love it," Grace says.

"I hope so."

"So we've been going through clips. I took the movies home last night. I know time is closing in to get this done. Christmas is next week," Asher says.

"I know. I felt bad telling Tate I had a full day of clients today, but I have to get this done."

"So, we aren't going to open for walk-ins?" Grace asks.

"I'm going to turn the sign at noon, but I kept my schedule clear today on purpose," Asher tells her.

If I haven't said it before, I'm saying it now—I fucking love my brother and sister-in-law. "Thanks, guys, really. I could not have pulled this off without you."

"You would have, but we wanted to help." Grace

stands and pulls a CD from her purse. "Last night we went through and found several small clips from a lot of the movies. We added them here." She hands me the disk.

"As Grace was going through the movies, I was looking for music to match the event, and that's all there." He points to another CD Grace hands me. "Certain clips of songs that match the movies well. It should be pretty easy to throw together. You have all the pictures you want to use, right?"

"Yeah, I have them all scanned and ready to go. I just needed to tackle the movies. You guys have saved me so much time. Thank you."

"Brandon fell asleep early, and he's still little so we didn't really have to hide it from him. We wanted to help. I agree with you that Tate doesn't talk about them enough. She's my best friend and I want her to heal. I want her to be able to talk about her memories," Grace tells me.

"All right, well, let's get to work."

I pull up the file that I've started and the folder with all the scanned pictures. I pop the CD in with the music clips and save it to the hard drive, then do the same with the video clips. Asher pulls his chair over and tugs Grace into his lap, and we soon get lost in creating my wife's Christmas present. It's not until there's a loud knock on the door that we realize we've been sitting in the same positions for the last four hours.

"Duty calls," Asher says. He kisses Grace quickly before letting her stand, then goes to handle the customer.

"Blaise, this is . . . amazing." Grace has tears in her eyes. "I wish I had this." She points to the screen. "The memories, proof of them. You are truly giving her something precious."

Grace had a hard life before she moved to Tennessee and met Asher. Much like Tatum, we are her only family. At least Tate has Leah and Brent; Grace was truly alone in the world. Reaching over, I place my hand on her knee. I don't say anything, as words aren't needed. She's been through a lot, but to look at her now, you would never know it. Grace is just that—full of grace. My brother is a lucky son-of-a-bitch.

Asher joins us a few minutes later. "Who was that?" I ask him.

"Walk-in, wanted a sleeve. Told him he would have to make an appointment."

Grace runs across the street and picks up lunch while Asher and I keep pushing through. By five o'clock I add the final picture. It's of me and Tate in the delivery room, the day the twins were born. I add the caption "Welcome to the world" and list their full names. I want them to understand the significance of where they got them. I click Save and exhale. It's done.

"Finished," I say, turning to look at Asher and Grace. Grace has tears in her eyes.

"Blaise. . . ." She shakes her head and gives me a watery smile.

"You nailed it, brother." Asher holds his fist out for me to bump.

"Thanks to the two of you. You helped more than you

know."

"It's Tate." Asher shrugs.

"So?" Grace wipes her eyes. "How are you going to wrap it up?"

"I don't know yet. I guess I need to think about that."

Asher laughs. "Well, you have six days. You better start thinking fast."

CHAPTER 10

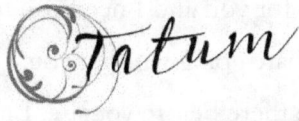

Today's the day, Christmas Eve, and I'm nervous as hell. The entire family gets together this afternoon at Blaise's parents to exchange gifts. I decided this was the day to tell him, when we are surrounded by our friends and family.

I'm trying like to hell to go on like it's just another normal day, but my excitement is getting the better of me.

"What has you all smiles this morning?" Blaise asks, wrapping me in a hug. "You don't usually smile this big while doing laundry."

I look over at the basket of clothes I just sat on our bed. "It's Christmas. The kids are really getting into it this year." It's not a complete fabrication of the truth. Stepping out of his arms, I take a big breath and go for it. "So listen, I have to run out in a little bit and pick up your gift."

He grins. "Waiting until the last minute, huh?"

"Not exactly. This is more of a . . . special order kind of thing. Just wasn't going to be ready until today."

"Now I'm intrigued."

"We have to be at your parents' at two, so I thought that you and the kids could just meet me there." He starts to protest. "B, come on. Work with me here. I have a surprise present for you and I need you to cooperate."

"Fine. I just hate going without you," he grumbles.

"Babe, I'll be there before you are. I just need a place to, uh, hide your present before you can see it."

"Okay," he concedes. "I love you, Tatum Richards."

"I love you too."

Blaise helps me finish folding the load of laundry and putting it away. I keep watching the clock. It's ten minutes to eleven. I really need to get moving so I can make sure everything is set up.

"Thanks for helping. I'm going to get ready to go. I'm going to take the food with me so you won't have to mess with it and wrangle the twins up on your own. I'll drop it by your parents' place before . . . uh . . . getting your gift."

He watches me, and I can see the suspicion in his eyes. He knows something's up. "You feeling okay?"

"Yeah, fine, just excited to get your present, that's all."

He nods. "All right, the kids and I will meet you there. Be safe. Love you." He kisses me good-bye and leaves the room.

I hear him tell the kids that Mommy's getting ready to

leave. I brace myself for them to enter the room. "Mommy, where you going?" Gavin asks.

"I have to get Daddy's present. Remember when I told you that you could help?"

"Yes," they say together.

"Good. I have a very special job for you. You think you can help me out?"

Their little heads bob up and down with excitement.

"Okay. I'm going to leave in a few minutes and pick up Daddy's gift. Once I have it, I'm going to call here and ask to talk to you, and then I'll give you your job. Can you handle that?"

"Yes!" they cheer.

"All right, but you can't tell Daddy I'm going to call. It needs to be a surprise."

Again they nod. It's not like if they tell him I'm going to call it will spoil the surprise. The only thing it will do is confirm my husband's suspicion that there is more going on than what I'm telling him.

"I'm really depending on you both," I tell them.

"We got this!" Gavin says, putting his arm around Addy's shoulders.

I pull them both into a hug. With a quick kiss good-bye, they head back to their playroom.

Blaise is in the living room, feet propped up on the table, watching football. He looks up when he hears me enter the room. "Hey, you." He smiles.

"Hi, I'm heading out. I'll see you guys there."

"Let me help you load everything up."

We go ahead and put all the gifts in the back of my SUV. Blaise insisted he could bring them, but I can be persistent when I want to be. He's not going to be thinking about remembering the gifts once I call the twins. "Really, I'll just drop it all off at once and it will be done. That way you only have to worry about you and the kids."

He doesn't argue, just loads up the gifts and sets the Crock-Pot on the floor of the backseat. I do the same with the cheesecake on the passenger-side and close the door.

"Be safe," he says, kissing my forehead and then opening my door for me. He waits until I'm buckled in before closing the door.

As I pull out of the drive, I look in the rearview mirror and he's still standing there. "Just a few more hours, B."

When I reach my in-laws' the whole gang is there. Brent, Jackson, and Asher help me carry in the gifts and the food.

"How did you manage to get away?" Asher asks.

"I told him I had to pick up his present. He didn't seem too impressed that I wanted to meet him here."

"I didn't think he would go for it," Jackson says.

"I wasn't sure he was going to."

"Here is everyone's card. You all know where you're supposed to be, right?" Ember asks.

They all agree.

"Tate, we're going to have Blaise leave the kids with us," Leah says.

"I was actually going to ask you that. I don't want him to have to get them in and out of their car seats at each stop."

"Once he realizes what's going on, I'm sure he won't mind. We'll leave right after to come here so we're here for the big reveal."

"Thank you." I look around the room at all of them. "You all are. . . . Thank you. I'm so blessed to be a part of this family." I feel the burn of tears. "Pregnancy hormones." I give them a watery smile.

"We love you," my father-in-law says. He wraps his arms around me in a hug and the next thing I know they all are. We're standing there in a huge group hug and my tears fall harder. The holidays are hard for me, but these people, my family, they make it easier.

"Right, so I have the bow and the shirt, and I even framed the ultrasound picture," Ember says.

"Now places, people. Tate, you'll make the call in fifteen minutes," Ember takes control. Thank God for my sister-in-law. I'm an emotional mess today.

CHAPTER 11

BLAISE

I'm sitting on the couch watching ESPN and missing my wife. I tried to get the twins to play a game with me, but they mumbled something about a secret mission and went back to the playroom. I can't help but feel a little rejected. It's Christmas Eve, and my kids and wife are otherwise engaged. The ringing of my cell phone brings me out of my pity party. Glancing at the screen, I see it's Tate.

"You miss me already?" I greet her.

She laughs and I close my eyes, savoring the sound. "Always, B. However, I called to talk to the kids. Can you get them for me?"

Something is up with her. "Sure. Just a sec." I pull the phone away from my ear and yell for the twins. "Gav, Addy! Mommy's on the phone."

Instantly their little feet come running down the hall. It sounds like a herd of cattle.

Gavin reaches me first and grabs the phone. "Hi,

Mommy." He grins. "Uh-huh, okay. Me and sissy?" he asks. "Okay. Love you too, Mommy." He hits End and hands the phone back to me. "Stay right here. We be right back." I watch as he grabs his sister's arm and they take off running. Not two minutes later, they come racing back into the living room with their arms behind their backs.

"Me first," Addy says. "Mine says one."

Gavin nods.

"Here, Daddy." My angel hands me an envelope with the letter B on it and a number 1.

"Where did you get this?" I ask her.

"Mommy left them for us to give to you."

Well, at least I know why Tate called. "Do I open it now?"

Addy looks at Gav, who nods.

I open the envelope and pull out the card.

B-

So this year, I wanted to mix things up a bit. I thought it would be fun to send you on a scavenger hunt to find your gift.

Merry Christmas,

Tatum

"Now mine." Gavin shoves another envelope in my hands. I stare at it and look back up at the kids. They're beaming with pride that they're taking part in this.

"Your mommy, she's a smart cookie," I tell him.

"Yeah," they agree.

At least it all makes sense now. I could tell there was something going on with Tate today. I've always been able to read her.

"Open it," Gav says, getting impatient.

I open the envelope carefully, just like the first, and pull out the card.

B-
I'll never be able to repay them for the love and support they've shown me. They helped me through the toughest time in my life.
They also brought me to you.
Tate

Leah and Brent. They brought her to Tennessee when they relocated. "Kids, get your coats. We're going out."

They cheer and run to get their coats on while I send Tatum a text.

Me: I love you, Tate.

Tate: I love you too. You have any guesses?

Me: It doesn't matter. As long as I have you and the kids.

Tate: Always. However, I think you're going to love your gift.

Me: Is it you, naked in a hotel room wearing nothing but a bow?

I see the bubbles pop up and then they disappear. Just as I'm about to type out another reply, I see the bubbles appear again.

Tate: You saying you want to unwrap me?

Me: Every damn day, Tatum Richards.

Tate: Noted. See you soon.

I slide my phone in my pocket and meet the twins at the door.

"We did good, right, Daddy?" Addy asks.

"Mommy said we had to keep it secret," Gav adds.

"Yes, you two are the best secret keepers ever." I open the door and guide them out to the truck. Once I have them strapped in, I head toward Leah and Brent's.

As soon as we pull into the drive, Leah, Brent, and Sophie step out on the front porch.

"Sophie!" Addy and Gav say in unison.

"The kids can stay with us," Brent says, walking over as soon as I get out of the truck. It's like he read my mind.

I don't know how many clues I have to chase, but getting the kids in and out of their seats every time is going to slow me down, and I can't imagine it would be much fun for them.

"Help me grab their seats. We'll take them to your parents' with us. We're actually getting ready to head over there."

"Thanks, man." We transfer the seats to their SUV and then join Leah and the kids on the porch. "You got an envelope for me?" I ask.

Sweet Sophie giggles and hands it over.

"Thank you, sweetheart."

I take the envelope and tear it open.

B-

I'll never forget the day we first crossed paths.

Tate

"She got you stumped?" Leah laughs.

"Nope," I say as the memory surfaces. "I know

exactly where to get my next clue." Bending down, I give the twins a quick hug. "You stay with Aunt Leah and Uncle Brent. They're going to take you to Grandma and Grandpa's. I'll meet you there."

"Okay," they say, dismissing me.

"Thanks again for taking them."

"No problem, man. We'll see you later," Brent says.

"You know, don't you?" I ask them. "You know what my present is?"

"Of course we do. Now go. You have a clue to find." Leah waves me off.

It's about a ten-minute drive across town to where Mom and Tate both used to work at the mayor's office. The office is obviously closed, today being Christmas Eve and all, so I don't exactly know where to look for the next clue. Maybe she taped it on the door.

When I pull into the lot, I see Mom's car and smile. I found my next clue. "Fancy meeting you here," I say, climbing out of the truck.

Her wide smile lets me know she's enjoying this. "I told her this one was too easy."

"They've all been easy so far."

She nods. "I don't think it's so much you figuring out the clues but the adventure that gets you to the end."

"You gonna give me a hint?"

"Nope. This is Tate's gift, and she worked hard on this scavenger hunt. No way will I ruin her surprise."

"Fine," I grumble good-naturedly. "You got an

envelope for me?"

She hands it to me and I rip it open.

B-

This place is important to your family. The man who used to sit behind the desk also had a hand in helping us find our way together.

Tate

I read the clue again before it hits me.

Dad.

The Firehouse.

"Thanks, Mom." I kiss her cheek and job back to the truck. The Firehouse is only two blocks over. Sure enough, when I pull in, I see Dad's truck. He's sitting on the tailgate wearing a grin.

"Took you long enough," he teases.

"Well, I had to get the twins ready, then transfer their seats to Leah, so you know, that takes time."

"You have any ideas yet?" he asks.

"Not one. I'm just following her clues. They've all

been pretty easy to figure out."

"Well, no point in keeping you waiting." He hands me another envelope.

I make quick work of breaking the seal and pulling out the next clue. My heart swells with love for my beautiful wife and excitement courses through my veins. I admit that I want to know what it is, what she's leading me to. I also don't want this little adventure to end just yet. The trip down memory lane is one we don't take often and I'm enjoying it.

B-

This is a place where you get to express yourself.

Tate

I throw my head back in laughter.

"What's it say?" Dad asks.

"I'm sure you know where I'm going next, but here you go." I show him the card.

"Self Expressions," we say at the same time.

"It's been fun, but more adventure waits," I say,

hopping off the tailgate and heading to my truck.

I'm fairly certain that I'm going to find my brother and his wife waiting for me at the shop. I glance in the rearview mirror and can't help but notice the smile on my face. My wife is full of surprises. This little adventure that she's sent me on is kind of fun. In a way, it's taking us through what got us to this point in our lives. Memories of how we met and fell in love that I will cherish for a lifetime. Quickly glancing over, I see all the cards of clues lying in the seat, and I know that I'll keep them. It will be a story for the grandkids one day.

Pulling into the lot of the shop, I see the lights on. I park beside Grace's SUV and head inside. Asher is sitting in the chair, Grace on his lap and Brandon on hers. The bell above the door catches their attention, causing a smile to tilt Grace's lips.

"Merry Christmas, Blaise."

"Merry Christmas."

At the sound of my voice, Brandon wiggles off his Mom's lap and comes rushing to me as fast as his little legs can carry him. Leaning down, I scoop him up in my arms "Hey, bud." I tickle his belly.

"My car." He holds up a pretty sweet-looking Hot Wheels hot rod for me to see.

"Nice."

My appraisal must be all he needs. He wiggles until I set him back on his feet, and then he heads right back to his parents.

"So, you got something for me?" I ask them.

"I don't know, babe. Do we have something for Blaise?" Asher asks his wife.

"Come on now, don't hold out on me. I'm getting close. I can feel it," I tell them. Not really. The clues really don't give me an actual clue as to what the gift might be; they're simply taking me on a trip down memory lane. Not that I'm complaining.

"Fine. Brandon, you have something for Uncle Blaise?" Asher prompts his son.

Brandon looks at his dad like he's lost his mind. Reaching around Grace, Asher grabs the envelope on the desk and hands it to my nephew. "Give this to Uncle Blaise, bud."

Grace sets Brandon on his feet, and he hobbles over wearing a slobbery grin and a smile as he hands me the envelope.

"Thanks, bud."

Placing my finger under the edge, I work my way across to break the seal. My reward is another card with another clue.

B-
You're doing great.
A family tradition that lights up the night sky.
Our first will be a memory I will certainly not forget.
Tate

Lights up the night sky. Family tradition. It hits me. "Fourth of July," I say to myself. The dock.

"Thanks." I wave the clue in the air. "I'll see you guys later," I manage to say before letting the door slam behind me. Tate said she had to pick up my gift and we were going to meet at my parents.' I have a feeling that this is my last clue.

CHAPTER 12

I'm sitting at the kitchen table with the whole gang, waiting on a text from Asher and Grace.

"You said he seemed to be enjoying it?" I ask his dad.

"He did. You have nothing to worry about, Tate. He's going to be thrilled."

My phone vibrates.

Grace: He just left. See you soon.

"He just left," I tell our family.

"Showtime," Leah says before standing. She helps me into my coat and hands me the wrapped ultrasound photo, making sure both I and the box are in presenting condition. "Beautiful." She squeezes my hand.

"I'll walk you down," Brent says, reaching for his coat.

"You don't have to do that," I tell him.

"Don't argue. It's starting to snow, and I would never

forgive myself if you slipped and fell."

I don't put up much of a fight. My legs are wobbly from nerves, so the offer to help me down to the dock is a welcome one. It's my gut instinct to refuse. They've helped me so much these last few years, and I still feel guilty.

After a round of hugs, I take Brent's arm and we head toward the dock.

"You good?" Brent asks once we reach it.

"Yes, thank you."

"All right, I'm going back up there before he gets here." He kisses my cheek and places the blanket over my shoulders—Leah's idea to hide the bow as long as possible—then turns to walk back up to the house.

I stand in the cold as the whisper of snowflakes fall from the December sky. I suck in a deep breath of cold air, then slowly exhale a cloud of white. I don't know why I'm so nervous; I know he wants this. We both do. Truth be told, I'm anxious to see his reaction.

When I see his truck pull into the drive, I stand up straight and turn to face the water.

"Showtime," I say to myself.

CHAPTER 13

BLAISE

I pull up to my parents' house and put the truck in Park. Leah and Brent are here, as well as Ember and Jackson. Ember walks out on the porch and I immediately spot the white envelope in her hand. Maybe I was wrong. Maybe this isn't my last stop.

Just as I'm getting out of the truck, Asher and Grace pull in as well. I don't wait for them, instead jogging up to the front porch to greet my little sister.

"Hey," I say, giving her a quick hug.

"You made it." She grins.

I chuckle at her enthusiasm. "I made it. You got something for me?" I motion toward the envelope in her hand.

"I do." She hands it over.

I quickly tear it open and pull out the card.

B-

Life with you has been beyond what I ever could have wished for.

With you, all my dreams have come true.

Thank you for loving me, for being my rock.

Now come find me on the dock.

With love,

Mrs. Blaise Richards

I'm man enough to admit that I was getting choked up until her little rhyme pulled me back. "God, I love her," I whisper.

"Then go get her," Ember says.

I hand her the card. "Hold onto this for me." With that, I jog down the porch steps and around the house. As soon as I reach the backyard, I see her. My wife is standing on the dock, facing the water.

I can't get to her fast enough, taking off in a dead run.

I need to hold her.

I slow when I reach the dock, knowing that she can hear my footsteps. I walk up behind her and place my hand on her shoulder. She turns to face me, her eyes shining with love and excitement.

"Hey, you," I whisper as I lean down and kiss her cold lips. When I step back, I notice the bow tied around her waist. A huge red Christmas bow. "Sweets, it's too cold to unwrap you out here. Not to mention no privacy." I wink at her.

"Funny story." She laughs. "This was all planned before you sent the text. So in a way, I'm giving you more than one Christmas wish," she explains.

"So what now?" I ask her.

She removes the blanket from her shoulders and lets it drop to the dock.

"Baby, it's cold out here. Put that back on." I bend to pick it up and she stops me with a hand on my arm.

"Unwrap me, Blaise."

I will admit that all kinds of dirty thoughts shuffle through my mind, but it's the serious expression on her face that has me reaching for the bow. I step closer and slowly begin to unravel it, never taking my eyes off her.

Once the bow falls to the dock, I cup her face in my hands and kiss her. She giggles and pulls back.

"What are you doing?" she asks.

"Kissing my Christmas present." I lean in for another kiss, but her hands on my chest stop me.

"You're not done yet. You need to open my coat. You *have* unwrapped a present before, right?" she teases.

"Babe, it's freezing out here," I remind her.

"I'll survive. Just humor me, please, B."

I bring my hands up to the top button on her coat,

slowly sliding each one through the hole. Once that's done, I look up at her. "Now what?" I ask.

She bites her bottom lip. "Open it."

I nod. Placing a hand on each lapel, I pull her coat open. Her shirt has a sparkly glitter package. I follow it, and there is an arrow pointing to her belly with words below.

Baby Number 3

My eyes snap up to Tatum. Hers are misty with tears and her smile is blinding. "Here." She hands me the package in her hand.

"Does this . . . ? Are we . . . ?" My voice cracks.

"Open it." She points to the package in my hands.

With shaking hands, I tear open the package and pull out what feels like a picture frame. Carefully, I pull back the tissue paper and suck in a breath.

An ultrasound picture.

"Tatum, I need the words, babe."

"Merry Christmas, Blaise. I hope it's okay if you don't actually get it until next August."

"Say it, Tate," I say again.

She loses the battle as a tear slips from the corner of her eye. I softly wipe it away with the pad of my thumb.

"We're having a baby. I'm due in August."

She's in my arms before she can finish. I crush her to me and hold her tight. "We're having a baby." Her words replay over and over as I swing her around in my arms.

"*Woohoo!*" I shout.

Tatum is laughing, tears still flowing when I finally set her on her feet. I tenderly cup her face and bring her lips to mine, kissing her until we're both breathless. Then I drop to my knees, pull her coat around her and slip my hands underneath. My cold hands cause her to shiver. "I'm sorry, baby," I say, looking up at her. *I just have to.* I raise her shirt and kiss her belly, then hurry and cover her back up before standing. "Let's get you inside." I gather the blanket, ribbon, wrapping paper and my picture and throw my arm over her shoulders. "Do the twins know?" I ask as we head back to the house.

"No, I wanted us to tell them together."

We step onto the porch and are greeted by our family. Hugs and congratulations are passed out.

"Let's take this inside," I say, pulling Tate from Mom's arms and leading her into the house. "Let's warm you up, babe. Both of you." I place my hand on her belly.

Another baby.

Best Christmas ever!

CHAPTER 14

"All right, you two. Brush your teeth and put on your jammies. We have to set cookies and milk out for Santa and then get in bed. He won't stop if you're awake," I tell them. Not that I'm worried they won't fall asleep; they played hard today with their cousins and all their new toys. They were just about asleep when we pulled in, but Blaise and I kept them talking on the way home to prevent it. It makes playing Santa so much easier when you know they're in a deep sleep.

"Can we have a story?" Addy asks.

"Of course you can, baby girl. Go brush your teeth and get some jammies on. I'll get the milk and cookies out so the twins can leave them for Santa," Blaise tells her.

"Kay," they say and rush off to do as told.

"Next year, we'll have a baby for Christmas."

Blaise wraps his arms around me and holds me close. "Thank you, Tatum. For this life, for our kids, for loving me. I wouldn't be me without you."

"I love you, B," I say, snuggling in closer.

"You too, sweets."

We don't move. I simply enjoy the feel of his arms around me and savor the moment.

"Ready!" Addy and Gav say, racing back in the room.

"Right." Blaise releases me. "Let's get Santa set up." He holds out a hand for each of them and they head toward the kitchen.

Once a plate of cookies and a huge glass of milk have been set out, we walk them to our room. "Pile in. It's time for *The Night Before Christmas*," Blaise says.

Addy giggles. "Daddy, it *is* the night before Christmas."

He kisses the top of her head. "That's right. It is."

Once the four of us are snuggled together, Blaise opens the book and begins to read. He's not even halfway through before they're out.

I slide out slowly and reach for Gavin. "Don't," he whispers. "You don't need to be lifting them. I got it."

I nod. He's right. They're getting too big to carry and with being pregnant, it's not a good idea. My heart aches at the thought. *How much longer until they feel like they're too big for Mommy and Daddy to carry them to bed? They're growing up too fast.*

Once Blaise has the kids warm and snuggled into their

beds, we head downstairs. "How long do you think we should wait?" he asks.

"At least an hour or so. I would hate for them to wake up and catch us."

He nods. "In that case, I think I want to give you your present tonight. I was going to do it tomorrow, but I'm not sure if you're going to like it, and it would be better if you didn't, that you not open it in front of the twins."

"It's from you, so of course I'll love it."

"I hope so. Come on." He laces his fingers through mine and leads me into the living room. "Sit," he says, pointing at the couch. I do as he asks and he covers me with a blanket before rushing to the tree and bringing me a small wrapped box.

"Open it." He looks nervous, which is silly.

I give him a reassuring smile and carefully unwrap the box. Inside I find a CD case labeled *Memories*. I open it and see a Post-it inside.

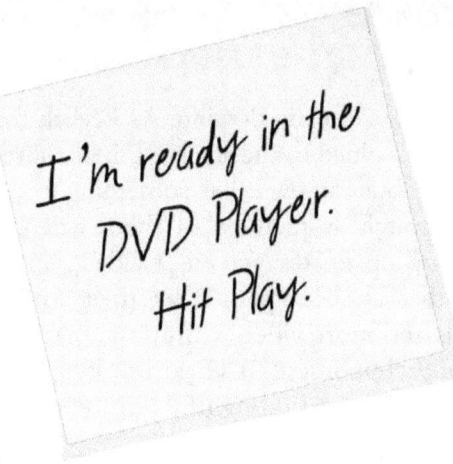

I'm ready in the DVD Player. Hit Play.

"Now for this next part, I'm gonna need you in my arms." He sits against the arm of the couch and opens his arms.

I slide between his legs and rest my head on his chest. Blaise pulls the cover over us and then sets a box of tissues on my lap. "Whenever you're ready, baby," he whispers, wrapping his arms around me.

Not knowing what to expect, I snuggle in and hit Play. A video of Blaise at what looks like the shop starts to play.

"Hey, Tate. I'm not sure how you're going to feel about this, so I want to ask for forgiveness now. This is something for you, for the twins. For our family. I know you miss this and I know this time of year is hard for you, but they are with you every day, their namesakes in our kids. I want them to be a bigger part of our lives. I want you to be able to talk about them and share memories. I know it hurts, but eventually as we do it more, it will get easier. Anyway, I just wanted to honor them for you, for Christmas. Merry Christmas, baby."

The tears are already flowing. As I reach for a tissue, I keep my eyes glued to the screen. I'm not sure what I'm going to see, but I know it has something to do with my parents. I watch as pictures of them when they were younger pop up on the screen, a video clip from their wedding that is accompanied by their wedding song. More stills and more video with music that captures the essence of each moment. It's heartbreaking and beautiful and the greatest, most thoughtful gift I've ever received.

I sit stock-still, his arms holding me tight, and watch

every second. When the final clip plays, it's a picture of Blaise and me the day the twins were born. Their full names flash across the screen, along with the date. The screen goes black and I immediately play it again. Blaise says nothing, just holds me while I cry for them, for me, for my kids, for our family. I let all of the pain flow.

Blaise is right; I talk about them occasionally, but not like I should. Not like they deserve. There are a few pictures of them around, so the twins know they are their grandparents who are now with the angels, but this, they can hear their voice, see them. He's given me my parents, our kids their grandparents.

After the movie plays for the second time, I sit up. Blaise does as well, waiting patiently for my reaction.

"I'll be right back." I stand and head to the restroom. I need to blow my nose and wash my hands. After I've cleaned up, I find Blaise on the couch, his elbows resting on his knees and his hands buried in his hair.

"Blaise," I whisper. At the sound of my voice, he's on his feet. In two long strides, he has his arms around me.

"I'm so sorry."

"Sorry? Why? You've given me the greatest gift of any I have ever received. I miss them. These tears are because I miss them, not because I'm upset with you."

"I know that, but I hate to see you upset. I mean, I knew that you would be, but I wasn't prepared for how it would twist me up inside seeing it."

"Thank you. I don't know how you pulled it off, but thank you. I can't wait for the twins to watch it. I'm glad you let me watch it without them for the first time, and the second." I laugh through my tears. "I love it, I love you and I just. . . . Thank you, B."

"Mine is still better," he says, kissing my temple.

"What?" I ask, confused.

"My gift." He places his hand on my belly. "Baby number three. We've made this life, Tatum, and it's in here." He places his hand over his heart. "My heart, it's you and our babies. I thank God every damn day for bringing you into my life."

He kisses me, sweet and tender and so Blaise. My husband, always the gentle giant.

"All right, let's get these presents under the tree and get to bed. The kids will be up early, I'm sure."

Blaise goes to the garage to get the bikes while I grab the gifts hidden in our bedroom closet. The gifts from us to the kids are already under the tree; these are just the Santa gifts that need to be put out. We work together to get them all under the tree, then both grab a cookie and share the glass of milk.

"Crap," I say, handing the glass back to him. "I forgot the stocking stuffers. Be right back." I rush to the hall closet and grab the small shopping bag with the stuffers. Blaise helps me fill them and now we're done.

"Time for bed, wife." He laces his fingers through mine and leads me toward our room. I change into my pajamas, wash my face and brush my teeth. Blaise beats me as usual and is already in bed waiting for me. The only light is from the glow of his bedside lamp. Something shiny catches my attention and I see it's the frame I gave him earlier today. My heart swells. *And to think I was worried.*

I climb into bed and Blaise clicks the light off. Immediately we meet in the middle of this big-ass bed. He wraps his arms around me, my back to his front. His hand slides under my shirt and rests on my belly.

"You want a boy or a girl?" he asks.

"Either one. I just want a healthy baby."

"Too bad it's not another set of twins," he says.

"Really?" I ask.

"Yeah. Gav and Addy always have someone their age to play with, and it was cool being a twin."

"Ember wasn't a twin and she turned out just fine."

"True." He chuckles. "Regardless, this baby is a piece of you and a piece of me." He traces my belly with his thumb. "We made this," he whispers.

"Hmm," I murmur, sleep starting to claim me.

I feel his chest rising as he laughs and kisses my shoulder. "Love you, T."

That's the last thing I remember before falling asleep.

CHAPTER 15

BLAISE

"Wake up, wake up, wake up," the twins say, bouncing on the mattress.

I force my eyes open and see that it's barely light outside.

"Santa came!" Addy says excitedly.

"Have you been to the tree?" Tate asks, sitting up and rubbing her eyes.

"No, but it's Christmas," Gavin explains.

"Well, let's go, then." Leaning over, I drop a kiss on Tate's forehead and climb out of bed.

"You too, Mommy," Gavin says, grabbing her hand and pulling her so she climbs out of bed.

All smiles, my beautiful wife goes with the flow and the four of us make our way to the living room. Tate and I sit on the floor, leaning against the couch while the kids take it all in.

"We got big-kid bikes!" Gavin cheers, racing to the blue one.

Addyson stares at hers with her mouth hanging open.

"What's wrong, baby girl?" I ask her.

"It's so pretty," she breathes.

I can't help but chuckle. "Go check it out," I encourage her. That must be all she needs because the next thing I know, she's across the room and climbing on hers.

"Daddy, we need to take off the baby wheels," Gavin says.

"We will, bud," I assure him. "Let's get some practice in first."

Tate has always wrapped the presents from us in "regular wrapping paper," as I call it. This year it's of a puppy wearing a Santa hat. Santa's gifts are always in the shiny, sparkly paper. It was something her parents did when she was little, and one of the traditions that we're passing on with our kids. I have to admit that it's a clear way for them to know who the gifts are from.

"Let's open presents, Gav," Addy says, climbing off her bike.

Gavin readily agrees, and they each grab a shiny present. Then the madness begins. They "ooh" and "ahh" over each gift and call out if it's from Mom and Dad or Santa, along with their thank-yous. The house is chaos, paper and ribbon overflowing and boxes galore.

As I survey the mess and the smile on my kids' faces, it's more than worth it. Once they're finished opening presents, Tate and I start breakfast. The munchkins requested pancakes, their favorite, so it doesn't take us long.

After breakfast, Tate and I sit on the couch and just watch them play. I love how animated they are. When they're finally starting to wear down, Tate surprises me, asking them to join us on the couch.

"You guys know Grandma and Grandpa Thompson are with the angels, right?" she asks them.

They nod their little heads.

"Well, Daddy got me a really cool gift."

I can already see the shimmer of tears in her eyes.

"I have something I want you to watch." She picks up the remote and hits Play.

"Daddy, you're on TV," Addy says, pointing.

I pull her into my lap and the four of us watch the movie.

Once it's over, I look at Tate and she nods. She threw the movie in on me, but we had already planned to tell them about the baby.

"Guys, we have something else to tell you." They both turn to face me. "You're going to have a little brother or sister."

"We are?" Addy's eyes grow wide.

"I want a sister," Gav declares.

"I just want a baby," Addy chimes in.

Tate smiles and wipes away the last of her tears. "Well, it's going to be a few weeks before we'll know what we're having, but you are going to be the big brother and sister. I'm going to need your help," Tate tells them.

"I can take care of babies," Addy says, squeezing her new doll to her chest.

"I know you can. Can I count on you two to help me?"

"Yes!" they cheer.

"All right, you two. Looks like you have some new toys to play with."

They scramble off my lap and dive into the pile of paper, laughing and giggling the entire time. Tate leans her head on my shoulder and I put my arm around her. This right here, this is living. This woman in my arms, she's given me this happiness. I think about yesterday and the test message I sent to her and the irony that I really did get to unwrap her. I plan to spend the rest of my life unwrapping Tatum.

8 MONTHS LATER...

Addyson & Gavin

"I want to hold her," Gavin says, stomping his foot on the ground.

"No! It's my turn. I'm the big sister," Addyson fires back.

"But I'm the brother. Daddy said I have to take care of her and you, so I hold her," Gavin says.

"Hey now, you two need to learn to share," Blaise tells them.

"But I'm the brother. I get to hold her."

"Listen, bud. Yes, you are the brother, and I want you to look out for your sisters, but you have to share with Addy," Blaise explains.

"But I love her," Gavin says, his voice softer.

"I know you do, little man, but Addy does too. You have to take turns."

Gavin scowls at his father but doesn't say anything else when he takes his new sister, Hope, from his arms and gives her to Addyson.

"We girls stick together," Addy says with a smile as she bends to kiss her new baby sister on the forehead.

"Both hands," Tatum reminds her.

"Mommy, I have babies. I know how to do it."

Blaise and Tatum chuckle. "We know you do, sweetheart, but we just want you to be extra careful."

Addyson nods and looks over at Gavin. "I'll teach you."

"I don't need you to. I'm the brother." He crosses his arms over his chest.

Tatum sits down beside Addyson while Blaise lifts Gavin onto his lap. "Listen, Hope is going to grow up with the best big brother and best big sister ever. Your mommy and I are hoping you both can teach her everything she needs to know. Gav, you need to teach her about your trucks and how to play ball. Addy, you need to show her how you took care of her when she was a baby and how to take care of her now. We need you to both share and get along. She's going to need both of you," Blaise says.

Both of them are quiet while they take in what their dad just said.

Finally, Addy speaks up. "Can you hold her, Mommy?"

Tatum lifts Hope from Addyson's lap and cradles her in her arms. Addyson then slides over on the couch and perches on her daddy's other knee. "I love you, bubby. We need to show her."

Gavin looks up at his sister and a slow smile crosses his lips. "Deal." He leans over and gives her a hug.

Blaise winks at his wife. "Number four Tate."

Tatum just smiles and nods. She can definitely get behind the idea of baby number four.

Jackson

After the presents that Blaise and Tatum got for each other this year, my diamond earrings seem lacking. I know Em is going to love them, considering she's wanted them forever, but still. I guess it's just because I'm envious of them. I need to start dropping more hints that I'm ready for us to start our family. I want a little girl who looks just like her momma.

"What's got you looking so serious?" Ember asks.

"Just thinking." I pull back the covers so she can climb in beside me. We just got home from doing Christmas at her parents' place.

"About?"

I motion with my head for her to climb in and she does. I snake my arm out and pull her close. "Making babies," I whisper in her ear before letting my lips trail down her neck.

"Really? Here I was hoping you were trying to decide if we could exchange gifts now instead of waiting until the morning."

I try not to let my disappointment show that she doesn't even seem to want to discuss it. "We can if you want. You know, when we have kids, we'll have to wait until Santa comes," I say, dropping another hint.

"No, we won't. Not if they're gifts to each other."

Damn.

"Be right back." I watch as she hops out of bed and races down the hall. She comes back carrying her present from me and mine from her. We went shopping together and got a few new things for the house, like the microwave for the basement and a new mixer for the kitchen. These two are the ones we picked out individually.

I'm just going to let it go for now and focus on the moment with my wife. "You go first," I say, pointing to her gift that is now sitting on the bed between us.

"You sure?" she asks.

"Yep."

She grins and slowly tears at the paper. When she sees the box with the jeweler's name, her grin widens. Slowly she lifts the lid and squeals! "Eeeep! Jackson! I love them, but, babe, they're too much."

I knew she would say that, but she's wanted them for a while now. Nothing is too much for her. "Not possible, Em. Put them on. I want to see you in them."

She gives me the look, the one that says she knows better than I do, but pulls them out of the box just the same. I watch as she places the one carat diamond studs in her ears, turning to the side so that I can see.

Leaning over, I nip her earlobe. "Beautiful, babe."

Turning her head, her lips meet mine and I get lost in the kiss. "Thank you," she whispers, pulling away all too soon. "Now your turn." She grins and hands me a small box.

It's tiny, and I don't have the slightest idea of what's inside.

"Open it," she says, her eyes locked on mine.

Carefully, I untie the ribbon and lift the lid off the box. Pulling back the layers of tissue paper, underneath is . . . her birth control pills? I look up and find her watching me, chewing on her bottom lip.

"So I thought that we could work on starting our own family," she says hesitantly.

Did she just . . . ? I look down at the pills and see they're missing up to today. I know she always takes them at night before bed.

Finally!

I toss the pills to the side and tug her into me, kissing the hell out of her. "Tonight? Can we start tonight?" I ask between kisses.

Ember giggles. "Yeah, tonight's good," she says as my lips trail down her neck.

Ember is everything to me, but to know that a part of me is going to be growing inside of her? That's deep. Soul-changing deep, and I can't wait for it to happen. To see her grow with our child. This is the next step in building our life together.

Unwrapping Tatum

I thought the day she agreed to marry me was the best day of my life. I didn't think I could ever love her more than I did in that moment.

I was wrong.

OTHER WORKS BY

Kaylee Ryan

AUTHOR

With You Series
Anywhere With You
More With You
Everything With You

Stand Alone Titles
Tempting Tatum
Levitate
Just Say When
Unexpected Reality

Soul Serenade Series
Emphatic
Assured

Southern Heart Series
Southern Pleasure
Southern Desire

CONTACT

Facebook:

www.facebook.com/KayleeRyanAuthor/

Goodreads:

www.goodreads.com/author/show/7060310.Kaylee_R
yan

Twitter:

@author_k_ryan

Instagram:

Kaylee_ryan_author

Website:

www.kayleeryan.com

ACKNOWLEDGEMENTS

To my readers, this one is for you. Thank you for your continued support. I love each and every one of you.

Cassy Roop Pink Ink Designs, you did an amazing job on the cover. Thank you so much.

Tami Integrity Formatting, you always take my words and create this beautiful display and I cannot thank you enough for all that you do for me.

My beta team: Kaylee 2, Jamie, Stacy and Lauren You ladies are my rock stars. I don't know what I would do without you.

Hot Tree Editing, thank you for making Unwrapping Tatum shine.

To all of the bloggers out there . . . Thank you so much. Your continued never-ending support of myself, and the entire indie community is greatly appreciated. I know that you don't hear it enough so hear me now. ***I appreciate each and every one of you and the support that you have given me.*** Thank you to all of you! There are way too many of you to list . . .

To my Kick Ass Crew, you ladies know who you are. I will never be able to tell you how much your support means. You all have truly earned your name. Thank you!

With Love,